THE COOK

THE
COOK

Maylis de Kerangal

Translated from the French by Sam Taylor

Farrar, Straus and Giroux

New York

Farrar, Straus and Giroux
175 Varick Street, New York 10014

Copyright © 2016 by Raconter la vie
Translation copyright © 2019 by Sam Taylor
All rights reserved
Printed in the United States of America
Originally published in French in 2016
by Éditions du Seuil, France, as *Un chemin de tables*
English translation published in the United States
by Farrar, Straus and Giroux
First American edition, 2019

Library of Congress Cataloging-in-Publication Data
Names: Kerangal, Maylis de, author. | Taylor, Sam.
Title: The cook / Maylis de Kerangal ; translated from the
    French by Sam Taylor.
Other titles: Chemin de tables. English
Description: First American edition. | New York : Farrar,
    Straus and Giroux, 2019.
Identifiers: LCCN 2018044068 | ISBN 9780374120900
    (hardcover)
Classification: LCC PQ2671.E64 C4413 2019 |
    DDC 843.92—dc23
LC record available at https://lccn.loc.gov/2018044068

Designed by Jonathan D. Lippincott

Our books may be purchased in bulk for promotional,
educational, or business use. Please contact your local
bookseller or the Macmillan Corporate and Premium Sales
Department at 1-800-221-7945, extension 5442, or by e-mail
at MacmillanSpecialMarkets@macmillan.com.

www.fsgbooks.com
www.twitter.com/fsgbooks • www.facebook.com/fsgbooks

1   3   5   7   9   10   8   6   4   2

THE COOK

Berlin

DONER KEBAB

A train moves toward Berlin. It speeds through wide-
open spaces, past smoking fields. It's fall. Sitting in a
second-class car, head leaning against the window, is
a slender young man, about twenty years old, travel-
ing light, a book in his hands; I am sitting on the
bench facing him. I decipher the title on the book's
cover—*La cuisine de référence*, the famous French hand-
book for culinary professionals—and see the three
stylized chef's hats drawn against a red, white, and
blue background, then I sit up and lean forward, pro-
pelling myself into the book's pages with their rows
of illustrations and italicized captions, step-by-step
photographs that feature no human face or mouth,
only torsos and hands: precise hands with clean, neatly
trimmed fingernails; hands holding metal, glass, or

plastic utensils; hands plunged inside containers, hands wielding blades, each hand captured in an action.

The young man leafs through the book's pages, consulting the table of contents and the glossary, the preface and the appendixes. He seems to be hovering around it without actually reading it, as if he didn't know where to start. In fact, I think he doesn't know much at all, not even what he's doing on this train on this day at this hour, and if you asked him the question, if you put him on the spot and demanded, "Why Berlin?," I imagine he would shrug, close his eyes, let his head sink back against the seat, and withdraw into himself. The only thing he is sure about is the fact of sitting in this car, immersed in its imitation leather and gleam of brass, in this atmosphere of confinement—damp warmth, detergent smell—his shoes touching this carpeted floor; the only thing he feels with any certainty is the steady power of the machine that carries him forward. A grayish blur through the window, the landscape is an old mattress; the boy closes the book and falls asleep.

October 2005, and it's freezing cold in Prenzlauer Berg as Mauro, travel bag slung over his shoulder, leaves the train station a few hours later and walks to a building on Lottumstrasse, where a friend of his has an apartment, rented for next to nothing, that will still be too big for the two of them. The staircase echoes, and when he reaches the landing, he finds the door open. Mauro enters, calls out—there's no one. He sits cross-legged on the floor next to a coal stove sculpted like the base of a fountain. He looks around: the large room is arranged with a few pieces of restored furniture. He rubs his hands, realizes he's hungry. He's here for three months.

⚹

All Mauro remembers of this Berlin period is the mix of cold, white, empty days and dark, hot, overpopulated nights—a balance that suits him. All the same, for the first few weeks, the daytime impresses him with its empty hours and its fibrous texture, like glass wool. Solitary hours in the apartment while Joachim— his roommate—works in a hip bar on Rosenthaler Strasse; floating hours where even the slightest movement makes the apartment creak, prompting him to turn up the music to its highest setting so he can't hear anything else. He chills out in this sonic cloud until the time comes for him to slip into another one—at the bar, where he goes to meet the others. There, he focuses on the gestures, expressions, faces, of those around him since he doesn't speak a word of German, and he writhes until dawn among the crazed bodies.

One morning, though, he stirs himself, shakes himself like a young colt. A small loaf of black bread, a café americano, and he's out the door. He goes out on reconnaissance, peacoat buttoned up tight, collar raised, less than ten euros in his pocket, and his gait now is that of a tracker on a hunt, as resolute as his path is random. The next day he goes out again, and he does the same the day after that. The streets in Berlin are organized clockwise: Pankow, Friedrichshain, Schöneberg, Dahlem, Charlottenburg, Tiergarten . . . Even so, he wears out his sneakers, his heels are covered with blisters, and when, from my window, I see him pass in the evening, on his way back down Lottumstrasse, I notice that he is limping slightly and remember a decoction of sage and green tea in which you can soak your feet to relieve the pain in the arches.

These urban wanderings are punctuated by brief pauses in the cafés of Neukölln to down a quick beer; prolonged pauses in the lines outside kebab shops at lunchtime, long queues where people breathe steam into the biting cold, where they stamp their feet, where they hop up and down, arms folded, hands wedged under armpits. The doner is a Berlin institution; there are more kebab shops here than McDonald's. Mauro will taste more than thirty during his stay, finally deciding on his favorite—made in a van at the Mehringdamm *U-Bahn* station. Crunchy slices of meat, sweet grilled onions, crisp fries, soft bread, the smooth sauce soaking through all of it, and hot, hot, hot: the perfect fuel.

These long walks are a way of orienting himself, of mapping the city in his mind, but they are also a way of giving himself space to think: while his body steams in the icy air, while he cleaves his way through the congested geography of a city in the midst of metamorphosis, it is his own life that Mauro maps out and orients, his own life that he elucidates.

Mile after mile, he goes over the past few years. The semesters in economics that he devoured at Censier until he got his degree, passing the final exams only by pulling an all-nighter, the sole burst of intensity in a year as transparent as glass, as soft as cotton wool; basking in the mud pool of collective sloth, the days veiled and the nights thickened by the smoking of joints, everything lost in a generalized haze with zero mnestic peaks showing through. . . . *Fuck, where did those years go?* The Lisbon parenthesis like a sun-soaked orange: the business school for young bourgeois heirs of the system, deserted in favor of an experiment in communal living, and all those roommates who were empty bellies, devoting themselves to four- or five-hour feasts consumed amid continuous talk, a confusion of tongues—Basque, Spanish, Portuguese, Italian—and Mia's tongue playing with his; Mauro cooking enormous gratins, lemon blancmanges, French toast, all sorts of soups and broths; the endless supply of homemade jams and farmhouse charcuterie, treasures wrapped in newspaper and smuggled at the bottoms of gym bags. The "comedown" with the arrival of summer, the end of the Erasmus course, the master's achieved, and it's bye-bye, Lisbon, the death knell of the lovers' banquet, and suddenly his life is a void, the future opaque. Then it's all poverty and brooding, and the car breaking down on the drive home, in the courtyard of a Charente farm where his cousin lives with Jeanne. It's midsummer; the countryside buzzes idly. For two months, Mauro does nothing. He has no plans, but he is sure of one thing: he will not go back to university in the fall.

At this stage of his Berlin wanderings, Mauro often takes a break. He goes into the first bar he finds, grabs a table near the door, and thinks about Jeanne.

A straw hat on her head, a pair of cut denim shorts revealing her sprinter's thighs, small rounded feet in leather ballet pumps, and a staggering workload—sheep, chickens, pigs, vegetable garden. He watches her as she crosses the farmyard, spade in hand, concentrating. He listens to her when she sits down outside the kitchen door and says to him as she rolls a cigarette: So, you're doing economics? Startled, he nods. He's leaning against the hot wall, holding a beer. Jeanne is interested in economics: she takes part in discussions on blogs, in forums, reads theoreticians of degrowth, studies new networks for organic agriculture. She smiles: Aside from the cigs and the wine, the vast majority of what we consume here is produced on the premises, hadn't you noticed? Mauro shakes his head; no, he hadn't noticed anything.

She is the first cook he meets. A professional now, she's been cooking for as long as she can remember. That summer, she shows him something beyond the gastronomical ingenuity of artists, which is the kind of cuisine he already knows, the kind done by friends who mix up their cultures. She introduces him to another realm—the realm of ecology, the territory of earthly resources. This is a vast expanse of fruits and vegetables: blond pears, speckled zucchini, new carrots and beefsteak tomatoes, tasty roots, elongated eggplants and wild herbs—chervil, sage, nettles. It is a continent populated by small poultry birds that you grab by the neck, where there's a pig called Napoléon, where the bull Soleil is king. It's a humane kind of cooking. Another world. Something is happening. Mauro loves how she lives, the way she thinks, connected to the earth, to the seasons; he loves her energy and the purity of her moods—sunny cheerfulness, stormy anger—and I feel certain that he was blown away by the assurance of her gestures, her gait, her look.

He doesn't go back to Paris right away, preferring to stay at the farm past the summer, working with the seasonal laborers and, in late September, leaving the Landes for Berlin, where he will meet up with Joachim—a way of extending this period of uncertainty. In Paris, Mauro stops by the Gibert bookstore in Place Saint-Michel, where he buys a Berlin guidebook and a stack of textbooks on cooking aimed at students taking professional exams.

⚹

That November morning, in the blue-aired apartment on Lottumstrasse where condensation streams down the windows, Mauro sticks an arm out of his duvet and plunges his hand into his duffel bag, waving it about inside as if testing the temperature of bathwater. This exploration, intended to bring him a few euros in change, leads his fingers to brush against the cold cover of one of those books on cooking, forgotten there, never opened. He takes it out and stares at it in surprise, as if he has just carried it up from the depths of time to the surface of the present. Then he gets up and walks to the Bibliothek am Wasserturm, on Prenzlauer Allee. At what moment, at what precise moment, does the course of one's life narrow, solidifying this particular path as a possible or desirable future, this path and not that one or any other? I often think that it was during this stay in Berlin—of which he retains only an impression of cold and of long distances—that Mauro began to emerge from latency, that kingdom of youth. And so it is that he finds a seat in the reading room and opens the book. The library is a modern, clear, calm place. It's warm in there.

2

Aulnay

CAKES, CARBONARA, HOMEMADE PIZZA

He had never considered cooking as a possible profession. Nowadays, everyone talks about the little boy
who used to hang around in front of the saucepans at
mealtimes, standing on tiptoes, nose in the casserole
dish, eyes riveted to the oven window, finger dipping
into the cream—What are we eating? What's that?
They like to remember the skinny, studious kid who,
having been given a book of cake recipes while still
in elementary school, spent the next few months
making one every day when he got home from school,
the way other kids might go to their bedroom to con-
struct worlds out of Lego, or organize cosmic robot
battles, or play PlayStation, or draw soccer players, or
read a comic book. These are the anecdotes that build
a legend, that help to create a logic along the lines of

"Even when he was very young . . ." Because, in truth, all that stuff about a calling, a voice whispering in the ear, a passion drawing the body forward in a firm straight line . . . there was none of that back then. I searched for some trace of it in his notebooks, his drawings, the letters he wrote to his grandmother at Christmas, but I didn't find any at all. At seven years old he wanted to be a circus clown. At fifteen he wanted to be rich, dreamed of bundles of cash, a classy international-playboy lifestyle—though he probably said this mostly to annoy his parents, a talented bohemian couple for whom this money obsession was just a phase, an awkward adolescent stage: they reacted with shrugs and wry smiles.

⚔

Mauro grows up in Seine-Saint-Denis in a family of artists—jack-of-all-trades father, sculptor mother, a younger sister. In Aulnay-sous-Bois, the couple found more than a place to live; they found a space in which they could create.

It's true, they're not rolling in money. Yet there is never any compromise in what is served at the family dinner table. The meals are delicious and varied; they don't eat just anything. Nor do they eat any old way:

the plates are flower patterned, the glasses tulip shaped, the cloth napkins rolled inside boxwood rings. What is at play during mealtimes is conceived as a relationship with one's body and an engagement with the world; the idea of self-awareness, or, in other words, what distinguishes humans from animals—Mauro's father, Jacques, recalls in his tenor voice that German has two verbs for "eat": *essen* (for humans) and *fressen* (for animals).

From the maternal—Italian—side of the family, the commensal culture of togetherness around a table brings a ritual aspect to each daily meal that is respected by all. What it also brings, alongside Anna—the adventurous, refined mother—is the sudden appearance of a grandmother, maker of legendary meals and walking repository of Tuscan cuisine, her recipes taken from the famous *Talismano della felicità*. From this point on, when the child enters the kitchen and ties a dish towel around his waist, he is under the dual influence of these almost polar opposites; or rather, as with all cooks, his odyssey is catalyzed by the continual friction between creativity and tradition, innovation and custom, surprise and simplicity.

To start with, though, the idea of creativity is dominant. That comes first, for the child, probably from seeing his mother, day after day, practice adapting and enhancing what she has at hand; seeing her use her resourcefulness and ingenuity to defy the constraints of tight purse strings. In other words, Mauro is taught the infinite variations to be drawn from simple, cheap products, with meat only once a week, and never a trip to a restaurant.

✕

From the beginning, Mauro enters the kitchen as if he were entering a magical sphere, part playground and part laboratory. There, he employs fire and water, commands machines and robots, and soon he has mastered several metamorphoses: melting and crystallizing, evaporating and boiling; the passage from solid to liquid, from hot to cold, from white to black (and vice versa), from raw to cooked. The kitchen is the theater of the world's transformation. In this way, cooking quickly becomes something more than a game with fixed rules; it is an object lesson, a chemical and sensory adventure.

So Mauro is ten years old when he starts on the cakes. Each evening, he throws his schoolbag across his bedroom and enters the kitchen. At that time of day he is alone in the house, master of all he surveys.

He probes the cupboards, makes an inventory of the fridge, then opens the cookbook and chooses a recipe that corresponds to the ingredients at his disposal, which he places on the table so that he can see them all readily. Next, he reads the recipe and visualizes the process. Soon he is pouring, breaking, weighing, beating, crushing, heating, measuring, decanting, manipulating, kneading, cutting, peeling, cooking, arranging, mixing, mimicking adult gestures. Soon he is making food for his family.

Because, right away, cooking entails other people; it entails the presence of others contained within the cake like the genie in the lamp. Because the preparation of a dish immediately calls for a set table, another guest, language, emotions, and every theatrical element of a meal, from the presentation of the dish to the remarks it provokes—the digestive rumblings of guests with full mouths and wide-open eyes. This is precisely where the pleasure lies for Mauro, who, as he becomes an adolescent, is known among his friends as the chef the way others take on the roles of the looker, the grease monkey, the geek, the brawler, the panty dropper, the athlete, or the joker of the gang— the gang in question being six boys who hang out together for seven years, through middle school and high school, without ever growing apart. *I've never cooked just for myself*—and he hands me a plate of octopus à la plancha.

⚶

What amazes me, from this era of patisseries, is the magical power of the cookbook. As if the cake resulted from the recipe, as if it came out of language the way it comes out of the oven when the cooking time is over. So that the more experienced he becomes, the more his vocabulary is enriched, incorporating the words of gastronomy. Following a recipe means matching sensory perceptions to verbs and nouns—and, for example, learning to distinguish what is diced from what is minced, and what is minced from what is chopped; learning to specify the different actions of boiling, broiling, poaching, grilling, sautéing, roasting, baking, reducing; learning to connect the array of colors, textures, and flavors to their infinitely nuanced counterparts in the culinary lexicon. Mauro acquires this language like a foreign tongue through a series of charlottes, babas, floating islands, marble cakes, cheesecakes, lemon meringue pies, bread puddings, macarons, pistachio financiers, Bavarian creams, crème brûlées, petits gâteaux, clafoutis, tiramisus, reines de saba, and other balthazars.

At the same time, Mauro trains his senses and is soon able to estimate by sight the capacity of a thimble, a teaspoon, a pinch of salt; he is able to gauge the volume and mass represented by 250 grams of flour and 50 grams of butter; knows how to adjust temperatures and cooking times, how to date an egg, a crème, an apple. Little by little, his sensations become more precise; at each stage of the preparation, they are mobilized as one, coalesced into a single movement, as if the boy himself were becoming unified; it's synesthesia, a feast, and now he can cook by ear as well as with his nose, hands, mouth, and eyes. His body exists more and more; it becomes the measure of the world.

※

As he grows older, the desire to amaze the adults at the family table—parents of friends—gradually lessens. Mauro has better things to do, teenage kicks to get, and the floor of home burns his feet. If he continues his incursions into the kitchen now, it is for his friends, and because it's better, cheaper. All the same, he does have principles: junk food is a form of violence perpetrated against the poor; the mass-produced ready-meal a sign of the solitude of urban existence. A thirteen-year-old ideologue, Mauro warns the gang: frozen pizzas are crap, and so is McDonald's. The friends say okay while patting their pockets and wonder out loud what could possibly beat the Big Mac Meal for less than seven euros? *Me!* Mauro jumps up.

Now on Saturday evenings, when Mauro and his five amigos turn up at the house in Aulnay, he immediately starts cooking, because the pure immanence of adolescent sloth—which is charming but also, let's be perfectly honest, pretty exhausting—requires its quota of slow sugar and its dose of calcium.

During those years, the Aulnay Six fuel up on "homemade" pizza, spaghetti carbonara, potatoes sautéed with shallots, chocolate mousse, crêpes suzette. *It's all right, guys, it's not expensive.* That's what Mauro tells them when they come to veg out at his house on weekends or after school and slump on couches while passing around a pot into which each of them chucks three or four euros—not including the Cokes, the beers, the smokes. They moan, they joke, and finally they devour what's put in front of them, silent except for the little sounds of swallowing. It's fit for a king.

After that, Mauro is responsible for the fueling of the troops before trips. *Stocking up, doing the food shopping, I've always loved that*, he tells me as he pushes a cart down the various aisles of the giant supermarket near Porte de Bagnolet, where I accompany him one morning: five thousand square feet, and he knows every inch of it. Unlike those—me included—who return every week to their local grocery store and scan the same rows of the same products, which they will buy in the same quantity, Mauro likes to move around, to explore, to amble. He is not numbed by the infinite variety of each type of food, by the packets of cereal in identical formats, by the multitude of butters—salted, unsalted, slightly salted, grass fed, cultured, clarified, clotted, organic, homemade, goat or sheep, packaged on butter dishes or in plastic tubs or simply wrapped up in greaseproof aluminum foil. On the contrary, he seems happy to have this multiplicity of choices. Soon, he slows down in front of the condiment aisle, picks up a jar of tomato sauce from the twenty or so on display, and holds it to the light, observing its color, reading the label—I watch him do this, waiting for him to speak—then he turns toward me and declares: *Tonight, we're going to innovate!* He knows everything there is to know about cookies, oil, rice, and is even capable of telling me the best brand of pasta to buy, depending on whether you're cooking a bolognese (Barilla) or an arrabbiata

(Panzani). I ask him if he figured out the menus in advance before a week's vacation in a rented apartment with his gang when he was fifteen, and he nods: *Of course, you have to have a menu, otherwise you're just messing around . . . And anyway, it's what I like to do, composing.*

3

Restaurants

TOURNEDOS ROSSINI

The first time he works in a restaurant, it is early summer 2004, at a brasserie named La Gourme, near Les Invalides. A summer job, which he got because his father knows the boss, paying a thousand euros a month. An opulent-looking place with a solid reputation: imitation leather benches in rose madder, tall mirrors on the walls, paunchy patrons with thin faces wearing charcoal suits and dark ties that are sometimes concealed by the large white napkins knotted around their necks like giant bibs. Not many women in the room—I'm the exception. Lurking in a corner behind a thriller, I am on the lookout for Mauro, waiting for him to burst through the double door from the kitchen, but he never appears; it is the boss himself who wanders around the restaurant, jovially greeting his customers, making jokes.

La Gourme offers a menu based on a gastronomic culture of quality craftsmanship: traditional recipes, generous portions, first-rate ingredients, not many surprises. The taste of continuity. The restaurant's philosophy is clear: here, the chef is at the service of the ingredients, not the other way around, and this sort of humility is polished to perfection with the delivery of seasonal produce. The customers, too, are regulars rather than adventurers, the kind of people who do not take many risks, who are looking for something they know, or have known, and come here to reactivate a sensory memory—terrine of rabbit with pistachios, seven-hour leg of lamb, grandmother's apple tart, or that delicately cinnamon-flavored madeleine, to be dipped in a light tea at the end of the meal.

A traditional establishment, La Gourme is one of the last restaurants in Paris to employ a butcher in its kitchen; every night, at about four in the morning, the boss goes to Rungis to bring back various cuts of red or white meat. Back at the restaurant, he places them on his butcher's chopping board, and they are prepared for the dishes offered on the menu. These exacting standards are the best kind of publicity: here, the meat is good, and everyone knows it.

So, that summer, Mauro discovers bourgeois French cuisine—another planet for this boy who ate his first foie gras at fifteen during a Christmas lunch at his aunt's house, and for whom the eggs in aspic ordered from the local deli by his grandfather for festive meals represent the height of sophistication—the edible capsule, the iridescent transparency, the delicate colors.

He's put in the Cold Appetizers department—in other words, anything that is served as a starter and does not need to be cooked afresh—and given a crucial post: the pantry, where the vegetables and the fruit are kept. He acquires a greater knowledge of them and is soon able to assess, by sight, the taste of a tomato, the subtlety of a stalk of asparagus, the crunch of a curly endive. Every day, he puts on a white apron made of thick, rough canvas that sheathes and holds him like a uniform, then he gets to work. The arrangements are simple, and—with the exception of the pâtés, which are presented in polished terra-cotta terrines—all the preparations are made on the plates themselves: tomato salad, herring and potatoes in oil, terrines of chicken liver chutney, egg mayonnaise, avocado and shrimp in cocktail sauce, a seafood platter. And the famous *mi-cuit* foie gras cooked in a dish towel, served with slices of toasted country bread, then swathed in napkins.

Mauro does well at La Gourme. He likes his job and claims that he hasn't experienced the tough side of life in a kitchen: the seventy-hour weeks, the authoritarianism, the relentless pace, the pressure. All the same, he's no fool: as the son of a friend, he was almost certainly given special treatment. Yet, despite getting his foot on the ladder, he does not imagine turning this first experience into a future career. According to him, he might just as easily have worked in a movie theater or a bicycle shop or a bank. He says he simply took the opportunity to earn a bit of cash before going camping with his gang, and while he had a great time—skillfully placing the two thick slices of foie gras on the plate without breaking them, then sprinkling the pinch of pepper and the pinch of salt onto them in two cones of the same size, with a spoonful of fig preserve at the center of the plate—he is adamant that cooking, for him, remains a passion, not a job. So, while the majority of apprentices who have graduated from a technical school would have tried to secure full-time employment after completing their apprenticeship, Mauro whistles as he leaves La Gourme, unlocks his bike, and—in September—

goes back to the round of economics lectures before, a few weeks later, moving on to the Catholic University in Lisbon, where he spends a year as part of the Erasmus program.

The second restaurant is a completely different experience. It happens two years later, in the summer of 2006.

The sabbatical year begun after the stay in Portugal is nearing its end, and Mauro is back from his foreign travels—Berlin, Italy, Venezuela. He moves into a studio apartment in the thirteenth arrondissement subleased to him by a friend who is away until September. He is in love with Mia, who has stayed in Lisbon, and spends a crazy amount of time online, searching for cut-rate airplane tickets. But the prices never drop low enough for him to afford a last-minute flight. He decides not to ask for any more money from his parents and to work all summer instead. He immediately starts looking for restaurant work: although he doesn't say it out loud, he knows now, he senses, that he could take that path, that he could become a cook.

So what makes him apply for unpaid work? I try to dissuade him one evening when we meet at the swimming pool, where Mauro, having forgotten the mandatory swimming cap, pushes fourteen gold-colored coins, one after another, into the slot of a vending machine, without having enough—I give him the exact amount. Why are you so determined to work for nothing? Mauro tenses, his face turns hard: he is thinking about the long term; he wants to learn, to train in the best establishments, and he's willing to work for free to do that. *Anyway, thanks for the advice, but I know what I'm doing.*

The Merveil on Rue Lamarck, at the back of the Montmartre hill, is the establishment in question: a hushed, conservative, luxurious Michelin-starred restaurant. The best in the north of the capital. A dining room for sixty covers; wood-paneled walls, tieback curtains, chintz, round tables with heavy tablecloths that reach down to the floor, white napkins, sculpted glasses, and silver flatware. The dishes there are precisely, immaculately arranged. So Mauro learns a new skill in the kitchen—meticulousness—and he learns it under pressure.

Initially, the young man is taken aback. Confronted for the first time with this desire for mastery, with this silent tension aimed at excellence, a tension capable of organizing the entirety of a team's work, a tension that can make a hierarchy dance, create a complex assembly of rivalries and micropowers that encourage and fight against one another, demand that the employees surpass themselves. A tension capable of building a system.

Above all, he enters a new world. This one is separated into two parts by a wall pierced by a double door; it is split into two opposing zones: the dining room on the street, the kitchen at the back. The former is a theater, a performance space, displayed before the eyes of all. Vast, lit up, serene. What strikes you immediately is its continual murmur: a calmness buzzing with sensations, looks, intentions. You hear whispers, the clink of glasses, the rustle of tablecloths and of fabric rubbing up against the backs of wing chairs; you feel the smoothness of bouquets of fresh flowers and the deep softness of carpets where high heels and leather soles sink; you imagine the exquisite presentation of the dishes, their sophisticated design, the pointillist line of balsamic vinegar on porcelain and the petals of beetroot chips forming a rose, the delicate little bowls containing miniature appetizers that melt or crunch in your mouth, the verrines with tie-dye shadings, the iced oysters scattered with petunias; you discover the flavors of those wines that slowly evolve on your palate, their taste that gradually overwhelms your entire body and creates a continuous sensual reality in which you dissolve; you visualize the softly lit room, intimate, rose colored, with just the right degree of shade for those smiling, pleasure-bathed faces unrestrainedly enjoying their privilege, obscene in their delight, while on the other side of the constantly swinging double door, behind the set, we find the second zone, governed by inverted laws.

Here there is no tingling silence, no soothing calm; this is a zone of noise. The whistling of the gas-stove fires, the grinding of blades, the thrum of small motors here and there, the popping of bubbles at the surface of broths, the metallic scrape and clang. Time does not flow here in sensory layers of liquidity; it is divided into minutes, into cooking times and presentation times punctuated by the voice that gives the order and by the bell that delivers the dish in return; space, too, is segmented, compartmentalized, each person confined within set borders, occupying a station; the chain of actions is painstakingly detailed, inch perfect, structured by obedience, discipline, the execution of commands: it is a military operation in which each employee is a soldier.

Mauro is disenchanted: people treat him like shit. They chide him, harry him. He feels as though he always has someone on his back, breathing down his neck, speaking into his ear. He realizes that in this place, words are merely a concentrate of rapid-fire instructions to which the only permissible response is a nod. They don't teach him much, either: it's up to him to adapt, to observe and understand; up to him to learn without slowing the tempo of the machine, without letting his inexperience and shortcomings affect the smooth running of the kitchen. You figure it out and you do your job. A situation that Mauro finds even harder to accept since he's working for free: to his mind, this is not a fair deal.

One morning, in the middle of a shift, someone whacks Mauro in the face with a metal melon baller—he chose the wrong diameter. Shocked, Mauro cries out, staggers, his nose bleeds; he stares around him in a circle, but no one meets his gaze; they are all busy working in silence. From his post, the chef yells at him to stop being a smart-ass and to do it all again pronto the way he's supposed to—it's not rocket science. Mauro loosens his fingers, lets go of his utensil—a potato peeler—then wipes his nose with the back of his hand, wipes his palms on his apron, pressing it against his chest, and picks up his knives, slowly washes them, carefully dries them, puts each in its sheath, unbuttons his jacket while around him some of the others now slow down, glance up at him—but without protesting, without stopping what they're doing—and then, still calm, he grabs his bag and crosses the kitchen toward the door, passing the chef, who turns his back on him and continues to act as if he hadn't seen anything, as if he never sees anything, until, as he is leaving the kitchen, Mauro dangles a hand along the work surface, knocking over a large stainless-steel bowl that clatters noisily to the floor as the doors flap shut behind him. I've seen him leave meals like that, classes, movie theaters, even girls; it's a manner of departure that is very Mauro: silent and determined, as if nothing could hold him back once he has decided to quit—nothing. On Christmas Eve, he will confide to me, as he prepares a chili con carne for eighteen people: *I stuck it out for three weeks, which isn't bad, really. I was too old for that kind of thing—I hadn't followed the usual path. I'd been through other experiences and I wasn't like the other apprentices. They were younger, all about seventeen or eighteen, more malleable, more easily intimidated.*

Outside, the sun beats down. Mauro is dazzled; he blinks, unlocks his bike, rides down Rue Caulaincourt without pedaling, freewheeling all the way to Place de Clichy. There, sitting at a table on the first terrace he comes to, he orders a ham baguette and a shandy and smiles, savoring the moment, free.

It's the middle of summer and Paris is full of tourists. There's plenty of work in restaurants, bars, and cafés, a quick turnover in the capital's kitchens. One week later, Mauro is hired as a commis chef at a brasserie called Les Voltigeurs in Montreuil. It's a permanent CDI contract—the first contract he has ever signed—at minimum wage. *In the restaurant trade, all contracts are permanent—it's always the cook who leaves, never the boss who fires him, 'cause they can never find enough workers!* Mauro squints appraisingly at a bowl of strawberries that he's just picked from the garden. *And minimum wage? Well, in a job where you're often working seventy or eighty hours a week, your paycheck at the end of the month doesn't really look like you're on minimum wage, you know?*

The restaurant is large: sixty to seventy covers. Two lunch shifts and two dinner shifts, served by a team of four people—*more sprints than the Olympics,* says Mauro, handing me a bowl of pistachios. It's not haute cuisine, but the ingredients are fresh, the setting pleasant, and Mauro gets along well with the tough Ariège-born owners—in the kitchen, two brothers of the same height and build, shaved heads, hunched shoulders, open smiles; serving the tables, their wives, two loudmouthed sisters, emotional and diligent, able-bodied, square jawed, with smokers' voices.

At Les Voltigeurs, Mauro is confronted with heavy shifts and a breakneck pace. He learns to deal with the rush hours, when no sooner have you finished preparing a meal than it is carried off to its table and you are already working on the next one. He grows physically tough, excels, flying from one task to the next, multi-skilling.

The two women treat him like a son, each of them outdoing the other with acts of generosity, saving him nice slices of calf's liver (full of protein) with raspberry sauce, a cup of meat juice to keep his strength up, and bowls of homemade, pastel-colored sorbets, but he doesn't touch any of it—no time, sorry—or if he does, he wolfs it down while standing in a corner of the kitchen. The women also squabble over who gets to look after him if he burns himself or cuts himself, the two of them standing side by side in the courtyard, preparing patches to help him fix his flat bike tire. Mauro likes them a lot.

Soon, he is spending all day at the restaurant, sleeping on a bench in the backyard, a cat in the sun, while the chefs take their nap, or—even better—seizing the opportunity to talk with Mia, burning up the minutes on his cell phone plan. Mia, who only answers one time in a dozen, and who can never speak to him tenderly, because she, too, is at work. In reality, Mauro doesn't do more with his break because he's too exhausted to move—or, rather, too worried about tiring himself out even more before he starts the evening shift—and he tells himself it would be stupid to waste his free time and energy on bike trips. So it's difficult to do the things he would like to do: to have a drink on a café terrace with a friend—me, for example—or to see a movie in an air-conditioned theater, or swim in a pool, or go for a boat ride.

As the summer wears on, Mauro stays at Les Voltigeurs for a good part of the nights, as the party continues at the bosses' table, where some of the more shameless customers often gather after the restaurant closes. Mauro hates those two-faced bastards, the way they squirm and say no, no, there's no need to cook them dinner, when, if they're coming here, at that time of night, it's because they know perfectly well that they will never be refused nourishment, the good stuff if possible. And it's Mauro who has to relight the oven that he's just spent a quarter of an hour cleaning, who has to take out the saucepan and the frying pan for a special omelet—Make them a nice mushroom puree, okay, Mauro? We can't let them starve, can we? The drinks, the jokes, the stories, often go on until about two in the morning, the bosses' laughter growing louder as the night advances.

One Sunday in mid-August, I meet up with Mauro in Vincennes. By the side of the lake, near the quay, we wait for our boat, sitting in the grass in the cool shade of an apple tree. He went to bed at three in the morning and he has dark circles under his eyes, the lean body of a marathon runner. He slowly licks his pistachio ice cream. By the time our brightly colored skiff arrives, my friend has fallen asleep, so I spend the rest of the afternoon reading my book, sitting close to him, waving away the wasps that hover above his T-shirt.

Mauro completes the summer at Les Voltigeurs, losing seven pounds while replenishing his pockets. But when the fall arrives, he tells the owners that he's leaving. The women's eyes widen, their jaws drop. They don't understand: Les Voltigeurs is all about continuity; he belongs to a professional world here, he has a place. They feel betrayed: This kid is so ungrateful! Mauro phones me in the evening to tell me about his departure, and I can sense that he's anxious, keyed up, and for the first time I hear him say that he can't stand any more of this grind, that these family businesses where you work from 7:00 a.m. to 2:00 a.m. seven days a week, they're just not his thing: *They're all too emotional—I'm not their kid! I'm not like them. I have a life. What I want is a simple job, normal hours, regular pay, you know?*

✳

September 2006. Mauro kisses the two women on their cheeks. They ball their fists on their hips and tease him, laughing: Go see if the grass really is greener, go on, but come back quick—this is your home! They calmed down when he told them what he was planning to do: go back to school, after his post-Erasmus sabbatical year, and earn a master's at the Institute for the Study of Economic and Social Development. They're impressed, they nod approvingly: the intimidating, coded world of academia is much easier for them to swallow than another restaurant.

Mauro's decision also comes as a surprise to his friends, who are beginning to find it hard to understand what he's up to: I mean, what's the plan exactly, postgrad studies or being a chef? He explains: going back to school is rooted in a desire to keep several irons in the fire, to spin several plates at once, like a Chinese juggler, so that he will always have something going on if one of the plates falls to the ground and smashes. He's probably also seeking to develop what is already quite an original résumé, which—he senses—grants him a uniqueness, an open-mindedness, the ability to think more broadly. In a way, the speed of turnover that he has seen in the restaurant industry encourages him to bide his time; he is confident that there will always be opportunities. He thinks he'll be able to find a few shifts to earn a bit of money— what he wants now is to go to Lisbon in November so he can be with Mia, hold her in his arms, breathe in the scent of her hair.

❧

Then another restaurant offers him a job. Mauro goes to meet the chef, who is also the owner. What's available is not a few extra hours but a full-time position. But while the rhythm of work at Les Voltigeurs stole whole days from him, as well as two-thirds of his nights, the hours here seem likely to produce a different outcome. In the fall of 2006, Mauro signs the contract—another minimum-wage CDI—and life speeds up again.

Le Villon is a small but sophisticated bistro on Rue des Petits-Champs. The three-course prix fixe is thirty-five euros, the dishes fairly basic but well prepared. Twenty customers at lunch, forty in the evening, but only one shift and a small team to keep things ticking over: two cooks, including Mauro, and an overworked dishwasher. The chef is a calm guy with bushy long black hair, a face like a knife blade, and sea-blue eyes sunk deep under the prominent arch of his brows. Mauro is immediately drawn to his modesty and intensity; enthusiastic, Mauro thinks that he will finally be able to experience, close up, the workings of a restaurant on a human scale. In the first days, after the physical exertions of the brasserie in Montreuil, he finds the workload here pretty light. Only in the first days, though. Because, from October, when the master's program starts to fill up his schedule, his days become crazily stretched out and segmented. He urgently needs to change his bike, to try something light—a quick, airy machine that will weave more easily through town. Mauro gets hold of a fixed-gear bike, pumps the tires to the limit, and speeds off every morning down Rue de la Roquette in the direction of Père Lachaise. From Tuesday to Saturday, his days are organized as follows:

8:00 a.m.–10:00 a.m.: master's, lecture hall, Rue de Bagnolet; 10:00 a.m.–2:00 p.m.: Le Villon; 3:00 p.m.–5:00 p.m.: master's, tutorial in Nogent-sur-Marne; 7:00 p.m.–11:30 p.m.: Le Villon.

So he has to keep going—maintain this pace, get through the day, not let things slip out of control. Doing that means accepting a life without any downtime, with no space to breathe except in the 5:00–7:00 p.m. slot, that two-hour late-afternoon break when he sits at a table with his Perrier with a slice of lemon to read in the silent back room of a café on Rue du Château-d'Eau.

His bike rides become moments of preparation during which he anticipates the next part of his day, goes over his to-do list in his head. Riding toward Le Villon, he reminds himself that he has to call such and such a supplier who didn't turn up the previous day, change a bulb, try the carpaccio of pear with slivers of Roquefort; riding toward Nogent or Rue de Bagnolet, he thinks that he must get such and such a book from the library, develop this or that idea in his paper, find a way to talk to this or that professor. Far from being exhausted, he wakes up more excited with every passing morning, galvanized by the idea of being constantly in action, as if enveloped by that idea, by the thought that he is someone who always has something to do, someone who occupies a place in the process, whose hours and days result in concrete actions and accomplishments. It's intoxicating. He barely even notices that his life—his social life, his love life—is drying up: the gang of six, his family, parties, movies, reading, days out . . . even Mia, whose face becomes more blurred day after day; Mia, whom he never went to see in Lisbon as he'd promised—no time, too much work—and whom he neglected when she paid him a surprise visit, leaving her asleep in the mornings and not seeing her again until the middle of the night, and by then he was too tired to lavish her with the affection she needed, too tired even to desire her, clearing his schedule for just one solitary afternoon so he could stroll with her through the backstreets of the quarter, without ever straying far from Le Villon, as if the restaurant were now the magnetic center of their relationship; Mia, who went back to Lisbon one day early, leaving a note on the bed, a short note, consisting of just a single word: *Basta*.

4

Blows

One evening, a month or two after the end of his time at Le Villon, we are watching TV, Mauro and I, in that studio apartment in the thirteenth arrondissement, which he has kept—though its Spartan decor still gives the impression that he isn't really living there. *Top Chef* is on. The French version of the reality competition show is a huge hit, as are all the other similar shows, whose ratings keep growing. The chef has become an important figure in contemporary society—a media star now remote from the grouchy guy who produced dishes from the shadows of his lair—and kitchens have become television studios. Mauro lists aloud the various programs—*MasterChef, Oui Chef!, An Almost Perfect Dinner, The World's Best Pastry Chef*—and I am amazed by how many there are. My friend shrugs: *It's obvious that when people talk about cooking, they don't talk about the rest, all the bad things going on in the world; it's obvious that people are always more interested in gastronomy during those periods when there's lots of anxiety: it's reassuring, it brings people together, it's about the body, about pleasure, it's about sharing, theatricality, truth.* Face darkening, he adds: *Competition, discipline, merit: everyone watches it, and it keeps them calm and happy.* On the screen, an immense kitchen scattered with multiple islands; the contestants stand in a row, arms crossed, listening to the presenter reminding them of the rules of the contest in a voice supercharged with enthusiasm. The goal is to create a dish around a pigeon. When the timer starts, the contestants rush to their countertops, in a panic, their thoughts scrambled, then each of them calms down and begins cooking. The pressure mounts as the clock ticks down.

Are you sure you want to watch this? I ask, surprised. Mauro doesn't answer, his eyes riveted to the image of those young people peeling, cutting, boiling. The stainless-steel utensils glisten in the spotlights; as does the food, which looks as if it were painted with varnish; as do the young chefs themselves, magnificent in aprons or in tight-fitting, dazzlingly white jackets. The camera lingers on their gestures, their meticulous hands, hands that seem to multiply like those of an Indian goddess, butchering a pigeon while simultaneously buttering a pie base. Drops of sweat bead on their faces as the countdown progresses, as the presenter talks with a famous chef, the two of them highlighting the contestants' qualities, their hard work, their hunger to surpass themselves, their heroism. Their teeth gleam as they speak. Suddenly, Mauro stands up, spitting acerbically: *Cooking is not the shiny happy world they're making it out to be; there's not much affection, you know*—and I can hear his teeth grind.

Violence is an old refrain in kitchens. Physical blows, thrown objects and utensils, burns, insults. The close quarters that exacerbate all contact, so that you push one another, knock one another over, so that you cannot stand your neighbor's elbow—Fuck off!—so that you defend your territory with your body, your square foot of space, so that you fight over machines and utensils. Stories emerge from kitchens: a commis chef who got punched for doing nothing when he was simply waiting for his saucepan to fill with water; another who got a plate in the face because the entrecôte was overdone; a third burned on the forearm by a spoon of boiling water or a red-hot blade because his beurre blanc wasn't up to standard; and other tales of newbies bullied, humiliated, hazed— I remember that apprentice who started before everyone else, to get ahead of the game, who woke up two hours earlier to arrange his plates, and the chef, furious at this attempt to evade his authority, who swept his forearm across the table, sending everything crashing to the ground. But most violent of all is that this violence is considered by the cooks themselves to be part of the job, an immutable law to which they must submit, an initiation they must simply survive. They talk about it as if it were a venerable tradition, even a form of education. To become a chef, you have to be prepared to get hurt. People who commit to this life are forewarned: they implicitly accept that they will suffer, resist, become hardened, support the idea of a natural selection that will eliminate the frail, the weak, the hesitant, the rebellious.

Obviously, this culture of violence goes hand in hand with a notion of solidarity that exists in kitchens. *It's kind of like a family*, Mauro says, without taking his eyes off the *Top Chef* contestants, who move about in a frenzy on the screen, and who, for now, do not share any brotherly feelings for one another. I smile: Come on, Mauro, not that old family line!

I wanted to remind him that not one of his colleagues had batted an eyelid when he quit Le Merveil after getting whacked in the face with that metal utensil, but he insists: *I mean it—the chefs often feel responsible for "their youngsters" as they call them; they look after them, they worry about them, and most of the time they're there for you if anything goes wrong.*

Yet he mentions another kind of violence: insidious, psychological. When a chef's demanding nature becomes a tyranny, an obsession. When the pressure in the kitchen is spread beyond its walls by those who suffer it, who activate its perverse mechanism, who sometimes preempt it and, in doing so, amplify it. It is this management through pressure that, mixed with rivalry, leads to things being blown out of proportion: *For example, when you arrive at work at eight a.m. as you were asked to and you find out that everyone's been there since seven, working flat out. So, the next day, what do you do? You get there at seven, too.* There is one thing, though, he makes clear, looking me straight in the eye: *I've never yelled "Yes, chef!" when I've been given an instruction or an order, never.* I remember a documentary on a prestigious restaurant in a famous Parisian hotel whose sound track might have been recorded at a military academy—West Point, for example, where

47

young men in uniform yell "Yes, sir!" in response to each order shouted in their face.

Mauro gets up and turns off the TV as the count-down continues on the screen—we won't find out tonight the identity of the best chef of the season, the name of the person who will pocket the hundred thousand euros and the approval of a jury of Michelin-starred chefs. Mauro turns to me and freezes: *But the worst kind of violence in this job, you know, the worst of all, in my opinion, is that the restaurant expects you to sacrifice everything for it, to give it your whole life.*

5

CAP

When he gets back from Caracas, where he attended the World Social Forum in April 2006 (he isn't especially impressed by Chávez), Mauro announces that he's decided to take the professional cook's CAP exam. The people around him are baffled, they don't understand: Why on earth would he choose the CAP (Certificate of Professional Aptitude)? In other words, why would he want the kind of diploma usually taken by the dregs of the national education system—people who will end up as manual workers, engineers, people who will never go to college—when he himself has spent years in further education and even holds a master's in economics? Seriously, if he does this, then what was the point of the Erasmus and all that stuff? His parents, anticonformist to the last, support him, happy that their son has found his path, but they make it clear that as far as they're concerned, this is his last year of subsidized study. Sometimes the specter of a loss of status rears its head, concealed under commonsense remarks: You're too old, Mauro, you'd be better off working, learning on the job. But Mauro holds firm: in reality, not only is the CAP a gauge of credibility in a professional world that is wary of slackers, dilettantes, middle-class shirkers fascinated by the culinary arts, it is also a symbolic gauge, the sign that he is willing to put in the hard yards, to accept the physical, technical, and prescriptive aspects of being a cook, to knuckle under its disciplinary requirements, to enter the tiled, metal-strewn backstage areas of the grand theater of French gastronomy—cultural heritage and national pride—and join the anonymous, invisible ranks of those who work in the shadows for its conservation, its expansion, its glory.

⚔

One year later, Mauro takes the exam as an unaffiliated candidate. That day, he puts on the chef's uniform that he must wear for the practical tests, an outfit purchased at Monsieur Veste for sixty-eight euros: white trousers and jacket, special loafers, chef's apron (down to his knees), and cap—he walks across the small garden, silent, the apron tied tight around his narrow torso, his long, thin arms hanging, and gives me a doubtful look: *Is this okay? Do I look like a clown or what?* I smile: he looks fine, completely credible. You look wonderful. After that, he gathers the utensils that he'll need for the test, an impressive array of gear that he inventories in front of me, picking up each object one after another and stating its name, a bit like a magician presenting his hat, his wand, and his assistant to the audience before performing his first trick: whisk, carver, peeler, scraper, zester, scissors, spaghetti tongs, meat tongs, fork, pastry bag with a variety of tips, rubber spatulas, an Exoglass spatula and a flat patisserie spatula, a ladle, several soup- and teaspoons, a melon baller, an electric scale (he checks the batteries), and a series of knives chosen after a great deal of research (the steel blades are laid flat in the black case, all pointing the same way—boning knives, butcher's knives, slicing knife, and paring knife, the sharpening steel). Mauro repeats their names, like a litany of weapons, finding it strange to be so heavily armed.

✄

The day of the exam, he is one of four unaffiliated candidates to turn up at the technical lycée in the eighteenth arrondissement. Apart from Mauro, there are two men his own age and a woman in her thirties. The exam room is large, tiled: the slightest sound creates an echo, but for now it is bathed in the singular silence of an empty school.

Having already dispensed with the basic tests—math and French—Mauro has crammed for the two other written exams: the PSE (Workplace Health) and cooking theory. The first is a general-question exam, about different contracts, the ability to implement a budget, or to react to an accident; the second verifies the student's knowledge of basic cooking techniques, of sanitary risks, the rules of hygiene, the organization of a kitchen, and so on. Mauro races through them.

The practical exam worries him more: each candidate has four hours and thirty minutes to plan and then prepare two meals (starter and entrée, or entrée and dessert) for four to eight people, to present them, and then to tidy up, while examiners observe his actions, note his techniques, assess the results. Mauro bites his lip and his cap slips down his forehead a little when he discovers the subject written on the board: old-fashioned blanquette de veau, raspberry zabaione. Meals he has rarely cooked; deceptively simple meals—the blanquette in particular is tricky, the success of the dish being entirely dependent on the velvety texture of the sauce. The countdown begins. He rubs his chin. Determined not to rush, he goes over to his workstation and begins to set up. The two other guys are also concentrating, appropriating their spaces, organizing the ingredients and utensils. The older woman, on the other hand, panics as she inventories her food—Monsieur, I don't have any carrots!—and one of the men gestures with his chin to a crate at the back of the room, without even uncrossing his arms. Mauro thinks, working out a plan of attack whose steps he writes down briefly in a notebook: the blanquette will simmer for three hours; during this time he will cook the mushrooms, blanch and sauté the pearl onions, and make the zabaione, which takes about twenty minutes. The sauce will be made later, with the broth from the meat. Mauro wonders for a moment how to deal with the raspberries and the cream between the meat and the mushrooms, imagining a raspberry blanquette and a mushroom zabaione, thinking that maybe they wouldn't be too bad, then he smiles, picks up the meat, places it at the bottom of the Dutch oven, and pours water over it. And that's it, he's on his way.

The four and a half hours of the test are incredibly rich and intense: the room is filled with movements and sounds—the lapping of the simmering sauce, the gurgling of the boiling water, the moist breath of the whisk in the cream, the *rat-tat-tat* of the knife blade chopping turnips, mincing carrots—and the silence is strained with breathing, exclamations, remarks, curses, and those encouraging little phrases you mutter to yourself to stay focused, to hang in there—Come on, that's it, come on! the young woman with the lopsided French twist exhorts herself in a whisper—so that the overall impression is of frantic agitation. The examiners keep their backs straight and crane their necks to peer at the workstations. From time to time, they question the students: Why aren't you turning down the heat? Why the Dutch oven rather than the stew pot? How well-done do you want it to be? Mauro gives the right answers, without losing sight of what he's supposed to be doing. He organizes his time as he breaks down the operations, crossing out each line one by one in his notebook, but somehow forgets to add flour to the sauce, which is too liquid on the spoon and messes up the presentation of his zabaione, damaging the raspberries so that their delicate shape is lost, their flesh torn, the cream stained with pink smears— Damn, it looks like a fucking fruit puree! When the time comes, he presents his dishes to the judges, who examine them before tasting them. Mauro waits impatiently, feeling wiped out and pessimistic. A beam of sunlight illuminates the freshly cleaned room; everything sparkles and shines. He is accepted.

6

A portrait

I want to describe this young man who is always hungry, who always wants to eat something, something good. This young man who is so determined and untamed. I sit on the terrace of a café in the eleventh arrondissement, facing the intersection, so I can watch him arrive. He bursts into sight on his bike, no helmet, his butt raised above the seat. The bike shudders as he brakes; he puts a foot on the ground and lifts up the frame, leaning it against the crash barrier that protects this stretch of Boulevard Voltaire, and quickly secures the lock. He does everything quickly, his gestures precise, inch perfect, as if choreographed.

In all honesty, he doesn't look the part. His entire being contradicts the cliché of the young chef who has passed his CAP: the white apron, pink cheeks, bushy hair cut short at the back and sides; the portly, jovial type. Nor does he fit with the stereotype of the trendy young urbanite who's all the rage in the *fooding* scene. He is lean, wiry, his triceps twitching—you need muscles in this business: cooking is athletic; it requires endurance, sprinting power, hurdling agility. What strikes you about him is his singular aura: the lightness and precision of his movements, the intense calm that makes him seem almost wise. He's fairly tall, with slender legs, narrow hips, and a flat chest, not an ounce of fat on him (just because he's young?); he has broad shoulders, it's true, but in profile he's like a stick figure. His face, too, is slim, with thin lips and soft, medium-length chestnut hair, round metal-framed glasses (a pseudo-intellectual? a young Trotskyite?) that give his eyes a gentle look. His skin is dark, his voice even. He has none of the expansive largesse characteristic of gastronomes—the wide smile, the laid-back hospitality, those people whose tongues love to taste and to talk, those show-offs with their smooth spiel, their gift of gab, their poetic speeches. He has none of their authoritarian presence, either, their tendency to rant, to bark orders. He is youthful, calm, saturnine, furtive. A cat. A Perrier with a slice of lemon. But what I need to describe are his hands. They work,

work all the time; they are high-caliber tools, sensitive instruments that create, touch, test—sensors. The fingers in particular are impressive: elongated and powerful like the fingers of a pianist capable of reaching three octaves for the right note, capable of unfolding in three movements, of dislocating themselves, capable of combining several gestures at once. A worker's hands and an artist's hands. Unusual hands.

7

La Belle Saison

GNOCCHI IN BUTTER AND SAGE

Four hundred thirty square feet carved in an old passageway in Faubourg Saint-Antoine: La Belle Saison consists of a single room, with a bar and regulation bathrooms. Mauro stands on the threshold, stamping his sneakers. His gaze slowly sweeps across the interior, the exposed beams and the tiled floor, the chairs stacked upside down on the tables. He assesses the place and nods, then turns back to Jacques, who is chatting with the owner: *It works for me!* Mauro's voice echoes in the passageway.

※

Ten months have passed since Mauro started at Le Villon. It's the longest he's held any job, and the partnership he forms with Pierre, the chef, is now well established. The two men understand each other intuitively—they're on the same wavelength—and eventually the young man is so competent at dealing with orders to suppliers, paying bills, and hiring dishwashers that he is given extra responsibilities, such as creating cold starters for the summer menu or choosing new plates for the restaurant. When Pierre is away, Mauro takes over without any decrease in quality. This starts to happen more and more often beginning in the spring of 2007: Pierre has fallen in love with a winemaker from Corbières who came to the restaurant to sell her wine. Now, whenever he can, he rushes off to join her in the hills where she lives, often spending half the week there, leaving Mauro to run Le Villon. The workload becomes untenable in June, though, with Mauro's exams approaching.

One Monday morning, Pierre pops in briefly to tell Mauro that he has decided to sell Le Villon and go live in Corbières. Mauro nods, stunned. It's all over within a week. There's no long goodbye.

The new owner is a handsome young man of thirty, cheerful and smart, who wants to create a restaurant that fits with the way the neighborhood is evolving: a stylish, pleasant place that will offer light meals in a cool minimalist decor—pale wood tables, inexpensive Eames-style chairs, and Japanese paper lamps, where people will eat soups, salads, bagels, quiches, pies, and the kinds of desserts that are popular with Brooklyn hipsters (carrot cakes, cheesecakes, cupcakes, doughnuts, brownies). Mauro listens to the new owner rave about this banal future, but Mauro is not convinced. He doesn't want to work in one of those places where the menu never changes, where there's no room for innovation; he doesn't want to work in one of these new tearooms for cool urban twentysomethings. He decides to wait, sees a few friends, and in June he obtains his CAP and his master's in economics. He knows that his profile is unusual, eye-catching.

※

Outside in the passageway, the December sunlight paints sharp shadows on the cobblestones. While Mauro looks around inside, his father, Jacques, chats with the owner, a tired old Lebanese man who recounts the place's history. It's been a focal point of the neighborhood for a long time. In 2001, when he bought it, it was an upmarket bar run by local personalities, with a small, high-quality restaurant, a good wine list, and cheeses and charcuterie imported directly from the producers. But everyone in the area still remembered La Belle Saison as a family restaurant where generations of local craftsmen went to eat, a lair of pleasure seekers that had up to ten different kinds of andouillettes on the menu; everyone talked about the tables set with checked tablecloths, the burlap curtains with red tiebacks, the reproductions hung on the stone walls—the still lifes in particular: the return from the hunt in the marshes, shellfish with a carafe of sparkling wine, a surreal Arcimboldo-style fruit basket—along with the certificate of good and loyal service awarded by the Association of Connoisseurs of Authentic Andouillette, displayed in a gilt frame next to a ham hanging from a nail. At one time, this local institution was serving a hundred covers per day—two seatings at lunch, two at dinner. Everything had gone well until the owners lost a lawsuit against their neighbors and were forced to get rid of the upstairs kitchen and somehow squeeze one onto the staircase. Without a real kitchen, and lacking resources, the restaurant was transformed into a high-end bar, and soon after that—hankering after a retirement of growing vegetables in Quercy after forty years in the restaurant business, twenty of them at La Belle Saison—the couple sold.

The current owner had just married a much younger woman and wanted to give her the bar as a gift. Together, for seven years, they had run La Belle Saison with the same clientele, who came for the labneh and baba ghanoush, the hummus and tabbouleh, and all sorts of grilled kebabs and meat-stuffed pastries of Lebanese cuisine. Today, the business is on its last legs, Jacques quickly realizes: there is still the problem of the kitchen on the stairs, and the owner is quite old. Running a restaurant demands an energy that he no longer has; he, too, would like to retire now.

Jacques calculates: the money at his disposal; the interest rate that the banks would agree to; the amount he could ask for from certain investors among his friends. The figures flash past. We should do it, eh? What do you think—shall we go for it? Mauro looks at his father, astonished by what is happening, the two of them standing side by side outside the front door of La Belle Saison, stunned that this idea, first mentioned three weeks earlier, in the kitchen of Mauro's parents' house, is now becoming a reality. That evening, in Aulnay, he'd cooked us a dish of cannelloni in cuttlefish ink, stuffed with ricotta, and dwelled on the thought: *Now, I'd like to open my own place!* We'd patronizingly warned him—It's tough, you know, running a restaurant, you're only twenty-four, you should enjoy your youth while you have it—and then Jacques had suddenly appeared and announced: That's a great idea, Mauro, let's do it together! At fifty-five, Jacques is energetic, garrulous, passionate about learning new things, and available—having just decided to quit his job as director of a computer science school. He has the time and the desire to create something. He raised his glass in a circle to toast this rush of enthusiasm, and I raised mine, too, looking at Mauro, who folded his napkin without any visible emotion.

※

Mauro stands outside La Belle Saison. He smiles. In a few days, he and Jacques will return to shake on the deal with the owner, go back into the restaurant, and open a cold, sparkling Anjou or, better yet, that old Château Kefraya from the Beqaa plain that they serve on important occasions. But for now, the young cook watches his father gather information, thinks to himself that this is a feasible project, not some outlandish fantasy, knows that he will have to work from dawn to dusk, and that even with the two of them, it will be a tall order. In the months after this, father and son get on with the serious task of financing the project. The banks are reluctant: the restaurant business is rarely profitable, more often a money pit, and the partnership leading the project does not look solid— all the same, let's examine it: The cook is young and unknown, he's worked professionally for less than a year, has no experience as a head chef, no knowledge of the culture of the profession; the father, meanwhile, knows nothing about the business. On top of that, the project requires a certain level of investment at the outset: the place is in decline, and they'll have to reinvigorate it—and that takes time.

Then there's the renovation. The kitchen is no good, and Jacques and Mauro are already planning to smash the wall of the staircase, move the toilets, and create a sort of micro-kitchen with four stove-top burners and an oven, a small work surface, and a mini-fridge. They will also fix up the little apartment above the restaurant, where Mauro will live. In the end it goes through: the financing is put in place, and in June 2008, Jacques and Mauro sign the deal for 150,000 euros. Just in time: one month later, the beginnings of the crisis appear—the big economic crisis of 2008.

The day before the opening, Mauro solemnly

invites me into La Belle Saison. We walk through the room, which seems to be holding its breath, and enter the tiny kitchen, where every inch of space has been assigned a specific use. He slides open drawers and cupboards, runs water from the faucets. I ask him if he knows what he's getting into; he looks me over and retorts: *I don't think about it, I just do it.*

June 18: the day of the opening. La Belle Saison is packed, the thirty-five seats accommodating a few extra people if they squeeze in a little. His friends are all there: the whole gang from Aulnay ordering bottle after bottle, the family, and the neighbors they met during the renovation. In his miniature kitchen, Mauro works flat out, everything so close by that he barely has to twist his torso, just reach out with an arm now and then to grab the ingredients and prepare the dishes. On the lunch menu, he offers a starter at six euros, entrées for between ten and twelve, a dessert for eight or nine. In the evenings, the restaurant serves crostini made with ingredients left over from lunch, which make delicate, original appetizers combining bell peppers and anchovies, pear and Roquefort, Brocciu and smoked tuna. Jacques, working the room, has found a platform for his cordiality, for the inexhaustible interest he takes in other people; as jovial as Mauro is silent, as attentive to his fellow diners as Mauro is to titillating their taste buds in the secrecy of his little kitchen, they make a unique duo who occasionally help out the resourceful, multi-lingual waitress—a friend who needs some extra cash. At La Belle Saison, it is always *la belle saison*—so Jacques announces to anyone who asks for details about the dishes when they order them.

From that first summer on, the restaurant is filled at lunchtime with a clientele of local employees and craftspeople who always take time out from their day to eat a good meal, even if they have to do it quickly, while the evening shift attracts foodies eager to dis-cover new "good little cateries," the kind of people who travel all over Paris in search of a good meal, ar-riving in groups of four or five to taste organic wines and elegant tapas. Word of mouth spreads fast, and by September Mauro and Jacques have decided to expand the evening menu to offer something more than just tapas—because the clients, it turns out, want to eat. A good sign. So things are going pretty well.

Back from the market, Mauro cooks without a break to be ready for noon, when the first customers turn up, empty bellied. What happens during those compressed hours is at once an intense improvisation, a high-flying sensory experience, and a confrontation with matter—natural, animate, extremely reactive matter. When I ask him to explain how he does it, Mauro shrugs, twists his mouth, and strokes his chin: *I focus on the ingredients: the idea is to reveal them, to highlight them. Sometimes, it's when you combine them with other ingredients that they show their true flavor.* These alliances, these contrasts, are his recipes: inter-pretations and reinventions of each vegetable that he brings back from the market. From time to time, he tastes the food the way a diver sounds the depths of the sea, trying to test the limits of what he's prepar-ing, the potential for expansion, for metamorphosis.

Nowadays, people talk about that pocket kitchen as if it were some sorcerer's lair, where Mauro, this self-taught chef from nowhere, brewed his potions; that little box room is mythologized into the beating heart of a magic factory, producing wondrous meals that changed and evolved day after day. Mackerel with fresh raspberries, sea bass with peach, pumpkin ri-sotto, beef braised in a carrot and basil sauce and served on a cabbage leaf, a sweet cake of potatoes with blood-orange sorbet, octopus salad with fresh fen-nel, rolls of sole and pancetta, monkfish tail with passion fruit, sea bream with spinach, pig's trotter and salmon-roe salad with fresh white-celery sauce. Some of La Belle Saison's recipes rapidly become signature dishes—notably the soft, melting gnocchi in butter and sage, or gnocchi with girolle mushrooms, or gnocchi with bacon and peas.

This inventive, delicate, unpretentious cuisine quickly wins admirers. Mauro's work is a reminder that, contrary to what many believe, the most gifted and innovative chef is not necessarily the one who transforms the ingredients, but perhaps the one who most intensely restores their flavors.

Rave reviews appear here and there on blogs written by food enthusiasts with powers of tantalizing description, people whose obsessive attention to detail suggests they live only for mealtimes: all of them salute the singularity of their experience at La Belle Saison. They are surprised, above all, by the chef's youth—twenty-four: a kid!—but also by his mastery, his sensitivity; what most impresses them is his temperament: savage, secretive, reluctant to enter the dining room, shake hands, collect compliments; a temperament that runs counter to the trend in gastronomy—cooking as a televised spectacle, a suspenseful contest, with the chefs transformed into personalities, media icons, faces that sell. Restaurant critics with hard-to-please reputations describe La Belle Saison as the most exciting discovery in years, and Mauro as a chef of great promise; hip bloggers, supposedly food crazy, publish photographs of their plates; the *fooding* community acknowledges him as one of their own—part of the new generation, the avant-garde.

In his first year, Mauro does virtually all the cooking himself. It's hard—physically difficult—for one guy on his own. He gets by with a little help from his family—his mother and his sisters lending a hand during peak time—and on little sleep, when the work he puts in would normally require long, restorative nights of slumber. A dishwasher joins the team, and he does a bit of peeling, but the kitchen is too cramped to allow any further recruitment. When it is expanded in 2009—a sign that something is really happening—Mauro hires a commis chef to assist him in the kitchen; he, too, has a minimum-wage CDI contract, but it really is minimum wage: no overtime—Mauro makes sure of that.

He decides to start earlier in the mornings, to prepare for the influx of customers who always turn up between 1:30 and 2:00 p.m.—twenty-five meals served in a frenzy. I ask him if the solitude bothers him, if he might find it easier to deal with the peculiar responsibility of delighting all these strangers were it shared with someone else, and he shakes his head, arguing that he is naturally independent: *I'm fine like this, I can chill out, I don't have anyone yelling at me.*

Above all, the day is long, very long. By the time the kitchen has been cleaned, it is 3:00 p.m. and at last Mauro can sit down. Take a break. He eats lunch as calm descends in the passageway, as if the air were suddenly thickening, swelling with silence. The restaurant empties; the commis chef and the dishwasher have now gone. Mauro relaxes, sometimes he falls asleep. Often, he goes back to the market to say hello to a few people, to have a drink with the other artisans, who are similarly haunted by these afternoon hours, these little lulls in their manic days, and then suddenly the afternoon is over: it's time to get back to the kitchen.

At 6:00 p.m., Mauro starts work again. He's already running late—he's always running late: *I've spent four years racing against time,* he tells me, preparing a clementine savarin cake in glass bowls with iced rims, in the middle of a heat wave.

The most difficult moment, curiously, is not the frenzy of the shift itself, but afterward, at night, when everything must be cleaned, put away, the tables set for the next day, that moment when the weight of the day lies heavily, when the stress has wrung you out and you are exhausted, too weak to talk or even look at someone. The commis chef and the dishwasher always finish before Mauro, who whizzes around until midnight at the earliest, when the last customers talk in whispers, order one last coffee as they put on their coats. It's the hour when Jacques launches into a long discussion with a local couple who are hanging out at the bar, and it's when Mauro, inscrutable, empties the trash, a signal that he will soon be going up to bed; this is Jacques's cue to announce in a solemn voice: Ladies and gentlemen, we are closing—there's school tomorrow, time to go home.

8

Aligre

JERUSALEM ARTICHOKES, CHUCK STEAK

It is eight in the morning, sometimes seven, when Mauro crosses the Rue du Faubourg Saint-Antoine. Then he is in sight of the Aligre market, carrying his basket or pushing his cart. The day begins; the vendors with stalls in the covered market and those with stands outside hail one another as they unload their goods and the first customers appear—shuffling old ladies who come for a conversation and their daily meat, three ounces of calf's liver or a chicken breast; busy mothers or fathers who quickly do the shopping on their way to work; and guys such as Mauro, who will serve about fifty meals in a day.

Mauro walks here every day now, come rain or shine, to buy meat, fish, and vegetables. It's the biggest moment of the day, the instant when the restaurant's menu is decided, depending on what the young man finds that is good and affordable—*Changing the menu daily, that's the fun part: you invent something new every day, you choose an "ingredient of the moment," so there's really no routine, for the customers or for me*, Mauro says, chewing on a matchstick while pointing with his eyes at some beautiful creamy white asparagus spears.

As a poor chef with no overdraft protection, constrained by a tight budget and with loans to pay back, Mauro still has to think about keeping his costs down, about haggling over prices. He can't go wild with his purchases. He has to exercise common sense.

This shopping is, more than anything else, the construction of a network of relationships essential to the smooth running of the restaurant, and from the beginning Mauro sees this daily outing as a form of learning, an endeavor that requires him to take his time, prove his credentials. He explores the perimeter, deciphers the circuits, identifies the different actors and the connections that link the places—who supplies whom—knowing that a restaurant such as La Belle Saison is a niche market of only marginal interest.

So, to begin with, he pays visits. He wanders along each aisle of the market, scans each stand, compares prices, assesses the merchandise, before finally spending time deciding who will supply him with fruit and vegetables—*You get a lot more bargaining power when you buy all the vegetables one guy is selling,* he tells me as we walk side by side. We push the shopping cart that has replaced the large basket he used to carry, but which became full too quickly, forcing Mauro to make two visits; the cart spares his back while increasing his purchasing capacity and strengthening his abs, shoulders, and arms—in the first days he will grimace with pain when he stretches and I will bring him some Tiger Balm, warning him to be careful: he's not supposed to cook with it. After a while, he ends up getting along well with a fruit and vegetable vendor who works hand in hand with a guy in Rungis whose task is to find him the best fruit and vegetable producers and to supply him with specific quantities of particular quality—forty-five pounds of new carrots for Mauro, small and preferably pointed, along with those rarer vegetables that he likes to cook with: Jerusalem artichokes, New Zealand spinach.

Beginning in 2010, Mauro works increasingly often with a new kind of grocery store whose raison d'être is to cut out the middleman between producer and consumer. The result is better prices and a rapid rotation of products, ensuring optimal freshness. Supplies arrive daily, precisely chosen. The products—fruit and vegetables, cheeses, charcuterie, fish and seafood—are collected by the grocer himself during regular trips to selected farms: he goes to Saumont-la-Poterie, in Seine-Maritime, to source the farmhouse Neufchâtel cheese; to Sarzeau, in Morbihan, for the filet mignon of smoked pork; to the La Croix de Pierre butcher, in Rouen, for the boudin blanc; to the Ferme de la Grange orchard, in Jumièges, Seine-Maritime, for Melrose apples and Conference pears; he will even drive all the way to the breeding ponds of Saint-Vaast-la-Hougue, on the English Channel, for the oysters. When he's not driving his van, he takes a cart onto a train and rides it to the last stop so he can fetch yogurts made with unpasteurized milk from a particular farm in Eure.

Meat is trickier. You have to join forces with a butcher you trust, team up with a supplier. The first one Mauro starts to work with closes in August, so—lacking funds—he decides to go to the Beauvau market to talk to one of the last few artisan butchers in Paris, a butcher with a stall whose prime rib, rabbit rillettes, and game meat are renowned throughout the capital. The man doesn't work with restaurants, as the quantities of meat they demand are too high—he refuses to put himself under a client's thumb and immediately makes clear his desire for independence, his determination to work the way he likes. I don't need you, you know, he seems to tell Mauro, who remains patient, going back to see him every day, getting to know him, hanging around the stall for a long time in the hope of an audience, a few words, a look of trust. It is like taming a wild animal. Mauro's stubborn persistence bears fruit: at the end of the summer, the butcher agrees to supply meat to La Belle Saison, an important step that will have implications for the restaurant's reputation. From this exchange, Mauro gains not only chuck steak that has been matured for seven weeks or fresh sides of veal, but a sort of symbolic anointing.

Lastly, there's the wine. It's difficult to come up with even a simple wine list when you have no culture of wine, that special knowledge that, it's said, takes more than a lifetime to acquire. Thankfully, in the daily socializing that often forms the first network of relationships in a neighborhood, Mauro will meet two guardian angels: Michel, owner of the Envolée wine bar, whose menu offers a good selection, and Fabrice, a sommelier from Bristol who works there.

Together, they organize blind tastings one Friday every month—*They're my education*, Mauro says as he beckons me closer so I can see in daylight the color of a Loire wine that he is turning slowly in a glass. Fabrice helps him choose the wines for his cellar. For Mauro, this is the moment to acknowledge that he is half-Italian: the wines of La Belle Saison will be organic, by small producers from his mother's homeland.

The question of supplies—a key one for any restaurant—is gradually fine-tuned. The trick is to combine freshness and reasonable prices with the available storage capacity—which, in the case of La Belle Saison, is extremely limited, with the mini-fridge already filled with all the dairy products. Annoyed by any wasted food, Mauro now works hard to find the exact quantities he needs. He tweaks the amount, tweaks it again, tweaks it until it's almost perfect, the evening tapas providing a tasty solution for the lunch leftovers. In this way, he does the shopping for only three meals, and no matter what, he is in the kitchen by ten o'clock.

9

Fatigue

After that, I didn't see him for four years. Or rather, I didn't see him the way we used to see each other before La Belle Saison: no boat trips on the shimmering waters of the Lac Daumesnil, no nocturnal cinema in Bastille, no swimming in the pool at Buttes-Chaumont, no lazing in the park, no evenings spent sprawled on a couch listening to music at his place or mine. If I wanted to have a moment alone with him, the only way was to turn up at the restaurant at the end of the dinner shift, between midnight and one, when the last clients were standing on the doorstep, congratulating him—It's art, Mauro! Lucullus Mauro! We'll come back every week, Mauro!—though without convincing him to leave his kitchen and chat with them; no, all he did was stick his head out and, wiping his hands on his apron, look at them, nodding with his chin while his lips articulated an inaudible *Thanks*. The dishwasher finished up, the commis chef put on his leather jacket, Jacques tidied the bar, Mauro poured himself a coffee and finally offered me a flat cheek: *How are you?* So I would sit on one of the stools and start to tell him; Mauro would ask for news about certain people, the gang of six and Mia, his ex-girlfriend—when I talked to him about Mia, something still seemed to light up in his eyes—but other than that, he spoke little, just monosyllables and half smiles, and after ten minutes he would turn on the computer to place orders at the grocery store on Rue de Charonne, clicking on multicolored files, typing in quantities of Gariguette strawberries or red kuri squash, so my words drowned slowly in the bluish light of the screen, until finally I would fall silent. One night, I ended up telling him softly: Okay, you're not listening, I'm going to leave, but he shuddered, as if shocked by an electric current, and put a hand on my arm and said loudly: *Stop—I'm shattered, can't you see?*

He calls me back six months later, one day in June 2012: *We're selling.* I'm dumbstruck: Shit, I thought it was going really well—"the rising star in eastern Paris," "a quirky cuisine far from the usual gastronomic poseurs," "instant, perfect, essential cooking"—and then I heard him laugh. *Don't worry, it is going really well—too well, in fact.* His voice sounds clear, less muffled than in my memory. He suggests we meet up, and one hour later we are sitting face-to-face in a bar in Butte-aux-Cailles, where I remind him that the last time I saw him during daylight hours was on New Year's Day three years ago: I was looking after a funny dog, which I walked as best I could near the Bastille. Mauro's not exactly glowing with health, admittedly, and the whites of his eyes are a little yellow, but all the same he is no longer the pale, paper-skinned ghoul who has spent half of the last three years on his feet inside a forty-foot-square cubbyhole. So, tell me. A Perrier with a slice of lemon. *I'm quitting. I've had enough. I'm beat. Bushed. Spent. Dog tired. Worn-out. Shattered. Drained. Exhausted. Out on my feet. Totally burned out. Listen, I'm fucked. I know it doesn't look like it, but I'm dead.*

I'm dead.

Fatigue. For four years, he's been tired. His back, his neck, his joints. Everything aches, all the time. He's forgotten how it feels to be healthy; no longer knows what it's like to live inside a well-rested,

83

pain-free, unstressed body; he's forgotten how it feels to be cheerful, to have free time, to live life with a hint of uncertainty. He tells me about his days spent chained to the daily running of the restaurant, to the control of the regular operations, to the perfection of a methodology capable of improving the meals he cooks; he describes the mental fatigue that mounts surreptitiously as his solitude intensifies, the solitude he feels with Jacques, with the commis chef and the dishwasher, that unshareable solitude of the boss, the *chef*.

I can tell he's getting carried away now; his flow of words accelerates, he bangs the table with his index finger as he describes the rhythm of work, the unflagging tempo that devours the morning, devours the evening—*That's the hardest thing: no evenings off, you know what I mean? I haven't had an evening off in four years!*—leaving just a few meager hours in the afternoon, a dead time that you could do something good with, but alone, because at that time of day everyone else is working, so you go upstairs to take a nap and you come back down when it's time to start work again, and on Sundays you sleep in, you stay in bed much too late, you just lie there, feeling groggy, because you're way too exhausted to do anything much with your time, so you hardly even leave the

84

neighborhood, and little by little the boundaries of your life shrink: the neighborhood, the passageway, La Belle Saison, the micro-kitchen where he keeps banging into things, until finally his entire life is reduced to the surface of that countertop. I saw again Mauro's studio apartment above La Belle Saison, the low-ceilinged room where he'd thrown a large mattress on the floor, where his clothes piled up, where the computer sat on top of a stack of unopened boxes of books; I saw again the orange sodium light that filtered through the permanently drawn curtains. Mauro lived in his workplace—I realized this suddenly—and what had, to begin with, seemed so practical—this little apartment, a convenience that would spare him so much time wasted on transport, yeah, he was so lucky—this little room had ultimately deprived him of any way of decompressing, had robbed him of a buffer between his workplace and his home, had stolen from him those tiny cracks, those hazy intervals, that can open up cavities of daydreams in the hardened concrete time of each day.

I'm dead. He laughs, leaning back in his chair, in front of me, hands crossed behind his head, eyes closed, dead. And four short words burst out of his mouth: *I want a life.* I observe him. Nearly thirty. Perhaps he's tormented by the idea of his youth rushing past him, wearing him down; perhaps he feels he is sacrificing himself to cooking, just as high-level athletes sacrifice themselves to sports—and we will never see it from close enough, that abstinence, that discipline, that suffering, the control of the body and the emotions that animate it, the mental life simmering carefully like milk over a fire, never boiling or spilling over, this order that is imposed on them and that they impose on themselves at twenty years old, this dark heroism straining toward glory. It couldn't go on like that forever, La Belle Saison. A gnawing logic, the logic of economics, the logic of business, demands, implacably, that you must grow if you do not want to perish; this logic insinuates itself into his life, like a current of cold air at the bottom of the ocean, before finally shattering when it collides with his youth. Recently—but was this because he was tired?—he'd felt that he was struggling to keep reinventing the dishes, varying the compositions using the same piece of meat without altering his methods, and suffering ever more from the restrictions of space— a general sensation of compression, obstacles, endless repetition. So he dropped out of the race; he folded. In doing this, he exploded the structure of time that bound up his existence.

10

Asia

POT-AU-FEU, BROTHS

Two months later, Bangkok is gray, lukewarm, fre-
netic. Mauro is working in a fashionable Italian restaurant where one of his friends, a chef, called him
about a vacant position. Mauro decided he wanted to
take off after the closure of La Belle Saison, and he
thought that Thailand would be a potential entry
point into the discovery of Asian cuisine. The sale of
the restaurant brought in 270,000 euros, a capital gain
that consoles him a little for the months spent without paying himself a salary; he has a little time to figure things out. For now, he is not working with any
local products: access to international cuisine is one
of the essential markers of the rich business class that
thrives here. And that's the milieu in which he's
operating.

He's initiated into the latest culinary trends, the ones that are all the rage in Los Angeles, London, Paris, and Dubai; he experiments with techniques that, before this, he had never even heard of, among them sous-vide cooking, which owes nothing to the bravura performances of a chef but is based on slow cooking at low temperatures, allowing a better concentration of juices and resulting in a tender consistency of the flesh. They're crazy about it in these prestige restaurants because it was developed by chemists who determined the precise clotting time; because it is infallible, leaves nothing to chance. Mauro is not particularly excited by all this: he considers this cooking method interesting only for the cheaper cuts of meat. It's perfect for a pot-au-feu, for example, cooked for forty-eight hours at 175°F, but ridiculous for a fillet of beef. On the other hand, he learns quickly. And starts to get bored.

One day, the boss asks if he'd like to work at another of his restaurants, newly opened in one of the city's most fashionable areas. The place has a radical concept: ten diners served a ten-course meal, open only in the evenings. The height of exclusivity and intimacy; the ultimate experience. This elitist idea creates a mimetic desire, similar to those provoked by limited editions and rare privileges: people are proud of having dined there; they think about it for a long time in advance, and the endless waiting list never gets any shorter. Mauro imagines it will be an adventure. He works hard, and everyone is impressed by his coolness under pressure, his creativity. But a few weeks later, when the owner tells him about his plan to create a chain of upmarket restaurants aimed at the global business class who travel to various cities on vacation, Mauro shakes his head: he's not interested. He can't imagine extending his time in this type of restaurant, has no desire to hang around any longer in this milieu of Thai society. He would like to see something more of Asia than this city, which has changed almost overnight from a paddy field to a luxury air-conditioned mall, this human anthill high on consumption, magnetized by the West.

His friend is surprised: What's your problem? There's serious dough to be made here, and the job's a lot cooler than it was in France, right? Mauro remains silent. He looks around: the pace is unflagging, but not frantic, thanks to the cheap, abundant labor force, who dilute the workload—*Imagine: ten guys to peel three carrots!*—and there is no management through pressure; in fact, a quiet calm reigns in the kitchen, the kind of calm that, if it cracks like a dry shell, if it breaks, gives rise to scenes of extraordinary violence: the meticulous commis chef slowly stuffing ravioli with ginger-glazed pork suddenly pulling a sharp knife in the middle of the kitchen and stabbing another man in the carotid artery while everyone else stands paralyzed in the steam rising from pans of broth. It's true that Mauro has an enviable position here: the restaurant needs him, a young French chef, for its corporate image. But he instinctively wishes to distance himself from something in these kitchens: something fastidious, something artificially enhanced, phony. You can see it in the gym-sculpted bodies of the cooks around him. A distorted view of beauty. So he leaves. He quits once again and continues his journey. Next stop: Burma.

He travels as a backpacker, adjusting his itinerary day by day, no longer looking for work, sleeping in people's homes. He discovers a secret, fiery, slow-moving country. Mauro strays as far from the beaten path as possible, staying in remote villages. The countryside is pleasant, a range of intense greens, his every step accompanied by a continual murmur. He takes the time to observe the movements of people preparing meals, in houses, in taverns. Here he will find what he came for: this street cuisine, this simple, popular cuisine distributed in bowls and tasted while one is sitting on little benches, those cooking pots bubbling with turmeric broths, all those fried dishes, those pickled vegetables, that cilantro-scented rice, those salads of tamarind leaves, of tea leaves, those dazzling fruits. He is amazed to discover these strange flavors that mix together deep in his memory, these aromas that he can't identify, these tastes that give him back his capacity for surprise.

I receive a postcard from him just before Christmas. A few words come back to me now: *ngapi, balachaung, ginger.*

11

Fooding

PORK RINDS, GREEN FAVA BEANS, PIGEONS

Mauro wanders. He's looking for something. Waiting patiently. I lose track of him for a few weeks, then he resurfaces, and each time we see each other he is in a different job, a different position at a different restaurant, as if he plans to learn everything, to experience every position there is.

I hear a rumor that he's a butcher's boy in Vanves, apprenticed to a man who is proud of his art; that he's learning to bone carcasses, to carve meat correctly, to prepare the different cuts; that he's learning to gut and clean poultry, rushing all day long between the cold room and the store, accompanying his boss to Rungis some nights—standing at the bar with the other butchers at five in the morning, drinking coffee and eating pork rinds on toast—and that he is learning the names and uses of the different blades with the seriousness of a Japanese samurai.

I locate him a few months later, working as a line cook in a three-star restaurant in the seventh arrondissement, hired by a big star chef. Under pressure, adrenaline pumping, he finds the experience interesting. He cooks vegetables grown especially for the restaurant in kitchen gardens in Sarthe or Eure, but he is definitely not a fan of the tension that reigns in the kitchen, nor of the fifteen hundred euros per month that he earns for his seventy-hour weeks. He lasts six weeks and then splits.

The following year, Mauro works regularly as the assistant chef in La Comète, a fashionable restaurant near the Paris Bourse. This time, he stays longer. The place is a rising star in the world of *fooding*: the chef is young and media friendly, and he worked in a famous restaurant after graduating from culinary school; the cuisine is in vogue, with its Scandinavian influences and its ingredients sourced from handpicked small organic producers. Seventy covers, twice a day. The concept of La Comète inverts the classic restaurant model: there is no fixed menu, and the dishes are directly inspired by the available ingredients: the three-course lunch menu is 45 euros; the six-course carte blanche menu is 75 euros; the same six-course menu is available in the evenings for 140 euros, with wine included. The interior architecture is open plan, with no separation between the kitchen and the dining room: a way of making the invisible visible—turning the cooks' work into choreography, a theatrical performance. A way of sharing what they do. The atmosphere is relaxed, a pared-down elegance composed of neutral colors and high-quality materials.

I want to see my friend at work, so I turn up one morning to attend the shift, the way you might attend a show. The team is young, international, a mix of male and female. The atmosphere in the kitchen is chill, hip, a little bit rock 'n' roll. Mauro told me about this: the people hired by La Comète had the means to create their own gastronomic culture; they are passionate about cuisine, a far cry from the mass of restaurant workers, who are essentially high school dropouts, kids who had to choose between being a boilermaker, a mechanic, and a cook, and who drifted toward the latter option. Mauro is paid twenty-five hundred euros per month for what are often seventy-hour weeks.

At eight in the morning, when work starts, nine, in addition to the chef, are in the narrow kitchen, divided between four workstations (one on meat, two on fish, three in the pantry, two on patisserie, and Mauro, the assistant chef). No one speaks. Everyone knows what he or she has to do—peel mushrooms and beans, hay-smoke the beef for the carpaccio, boil (but not blanch) the fava beans. At ten o'clock, the tempo accelerates in a way that is barely perceptible. Voices are raised—Have you gutted the fish yet? How's the turbot? Can you bring me six pounds of cream?—and the cooks chat about the latest news: who's leaving, who's just joined, an assistant chef who's got a chef's position down south, that brilliant sommelier who's quitting his job to live in Chile, that new restaurant opening in Ménilmontant—So? What's it like? They compare jobs, wages, hours, contrast the reputations of different restaurants, different chefs. At eleven, everyone stops: it's time to clean up. The kitchen is made beautiful again, ready for the lunch shift. The employees assiduously scrub an area of their workstation, leaning over the stove top, stretching an arm across the stainless-steel surface, exposing the top of their underwear and a strip of flesh if possible. Perforated rubber mats are laid out everywhere. After that, the pace accelerates gradually, and when it finally starts, it's a thing of beauty: rapid and fluid, rhythmic and precise, the plates whisked away one after another with each announcement. The rush starts around one thirty and the intensity goes up a notch; concentration is at its height; this is the moment when the precisely calibrated choreography most impresses the watching diners. When at last it slows down again, it's nearly three. The dishwashers have cleaned nearly 420 plates because the restaurant was full, and I hear a familiar voice ask out loud: *So, what are we going to cook tomorrow?*

12

Suckling pig

Mauro quits his job at La Comète at the start of the summer, but goes back to work there occasionally, sometimes replacing the chef when he's away. In the months that follow, he uses his free time and his freedom of movement to rack up experience: he works briefly as an adviser for a new kind of café chain offering hot and cold meals, and moonlights at ten euros per hour for a friend when she's preparing to cook for a table of ten in a private restaurant in the Marais for a month, as a way of getting better known. He has something on his mind, I can tell. I ask him about it one summer night as we're walking down Rue des Envierges toward the Parc de Belleville. *I'd like to open another restaurant.* I stop dead on the sidewalk. Along the same lines as La Belle Saison? I ask. He shakes his head. Not really. The idea is to create a place that will give back importance to what's happening in the dining room. A restaurant that will reinvent the notion of the commensal—togetherness around a table. The concept is that the meal will not only express the glorious creativity of one person, will not only provide an individual sensory experience, but will be about relationships, a possible collective adventure. *Like, you want to eat a roast suckling pig, but it's a meal for four or five people, so you stand up and you ask if anyone would like to share a suckling pig with you. Then you go over to the other person's table, you talk with him, and that's how it starts. You see?* I see. I smile and pretend to hand him my plate.

A NOTE ABOUT THE AUTHOR

Maylis de Kerangal is the author of several novels: *Je marche sous un ciel de traîne* (2000), *La vie voyageuse* (2003), *Corniche Kennedy* (2008), and *Naissance d'un pont* (winner of the Prix Franz Hessel and the Prix Médicis in 2010; published in English as *Birth of a Bridge*). In 2014, her fifth novel, *Réparer les vivants* (published in the United States in 2016 as *The Heart*), received wide acclaim and won the Grand Prix RTL-Lire and the Student Choice Novel of the Year from France Culture and Télérama. She lives in Paris.

A NOTE ABOUT THE TRANSLATOR

Sam Taylor is the author of three novels and has translated more than thirty books from the French, including Laurent Binet's *HHhH*, Leila Slimani's *The Perfect Nanny*, and Joel Dicker's *The Truth About the Harry Quebert Affair*. His translation of Maylis de Kerangal's *The Heart* won the French-American Foundation's Translation Prize and the Lewis Galantière Award.